A SAGEBRUSH CINDERELLA

Max Brand

Pharos Books

ISBN: 978-93-58047-72-1
eISBN: 978-93-58047-67-7

©Publisher

Publisher: Pharos Books (P) Ltd.
Plot No.-55, Main Mother Dairy Road
Pandav Nagar, East Delhi-110092
Phone: 011-40395855, +4049916623
WhatsApp: +91 8368220032
E-mail: sales@pharosbooks.in
Website: www.pharosbooks.in
First Edition: 2022

A SAGEBRUSH CINDERELLA
By Max Brand

CONTENTS

A SAGEBRUSH CINDERELLA

CHAPTER I

WHISKERS

She lay prone upon the floor, kicking her heels together, frowningly intent upon her book. Outside the sky was crimson with the sunset. Inside the room, every corner was filled with the gay fantoms of the age of chivalry. Jac would not raise her head, for if she kept her eyes upon the printed page it seemed to her that the armored knights were trooping about her rooms. A board creaked. That was from the running of some striped page with pointed toes. The wind made a soft rustling. That was the stir of the nodding plumes of the warriors. The pageantry of forgotten kings flowed brightly about her.

"Jac!"

Jacqueline frowned and shrugged her shoulders.

"Jac!"

She raised her head. The dreary board walls of her room looked back at her, empty, barren, a thousand miles and a thousand years from all romance. She closed her book as the door of her room opened and her father stood in the entrance.

"Readin' again!" said Jim During in infinite disgust. "Go down an' wait on the table. The cook's gone an' got drunk. I've give him the run. Hurry up."

She shied the book into a corner and rose.

"How many here for chow?" she asked.

"Maurice Gordon an' a lot of others," said her father. "Start movin'!"

She started. Handsome Maurice Gordon! She had only to close her eyes and there he stood in armor—Sir Maurice de Gordon!

You might have combed the cattle ranges for five hundred miles north, east, south, and west, and never found so fine a figure of a man as Maurice Gordon. Good looks are rather a handicap than a blessing in the mountain desert, but "Maurie" Gordon was notably ready at all times for anything from a dance to a fight, and his reputation was accordingly as high among men as among women.

He made a stir wherever he went, and now as he sat in the dining-room of Jim During's crossroads hotel, all eyes were upon him. He withstood their critical admiration with the nonchalant good-nature of one who knew that, from his silk bandanna to his fine riding-boots, his outfit represented the beau-ideal of the cow-puncher.

"Where you bound for?" asked the proprietor of the hotel as the supper drew toward its close.

"The dance over to Bridewell," said Maurie. "Damnation!"

For as he mentioned the dance, Jac, who was bringing him his second cup of coffee, started so violently that a drop of the hot liquid splashed on the back of Maurie's neck.

"Oh!" she cried, and seized her apron to wipe away the coffee.

"'Scuse me," growled Maurie, seeing that he had sworn at a woman. "But you took me by surprise."

With that he stopped the hand which was bearing the soiled apron toward his neck, and produced from his pocket—marvelous to behold!—a handkerchief of stainless white, with which he rubbed away the coffee.

"Jacqueline!" rumbled her father, and his accent made the name far more emphatic than Maurie's "damnation."

That was her given title, but to every cow-puncher on the ranges she was known as "Jac" During, who rode, shot, and sometimes swore as well as any man of them all. She was Jacqueline to her father alone, and to him only at such a time as this.

　　　　　　　　　　　　　　A SAGEBRUSH CINDERELLA

"Well?" she said belligerently, and her eyes fixed on her father as steadily and as angrily as those of a man.

"Your hands was made for feet! Go back to the kitchen. We don't need you till the boys is through with their coffee. Too bad, Maurie."

"Nothin' at all!" said the latter heartily, and waved the matter out of existence.

He might banish Jac from his thoughts with a gesture, but he could not drive away her thoughts of him so easily, it seemed; for she stopped in the shadow of the doorway which led into the kitchen and stared back with big eyes at the cow-puncher.

"Who you takin' to the dance?" said her father.

"Dolly Maxwell," said Maurie, naming the prettiest girl in many, many miles.

"That pale-faced—thing!" muttered Jac, relapsing into a feminine vocabulary at this crisis. But she sighed as she turned back into the kitchen.

She threw open the door of the stove so that the light flamed on her red hair, which was tied in a hard knot on top of her head—the quickest, easiest, and unquestionably the most ugly manner of dressing hair. A vast and unreasoning rage made her blood hot.

The anger was partly for her own blunder in spilling the hot coffee. It was even more because of Maurie's ejaculation. With that one word he had banished the vision of Sir Maurice de Gordon. The plumed helmet had fallen from his head; his bright armor had blown away on a gust of reality. In the fury of her chagrin Jac caught up the poker and raked the grate of the stove loudly. The rattling helped to relieve her as swearing, perhaps, relieves a man. In the midst of the racket she heard a chuckle from the dining-room, and her blood went cold at the thought that some one might understand the deeps of her shame and wrath.

She ran to the door. There she sighed again, but it was relief this time. At least it was not Maurie who laughed. He was deep in conversation with his neighbor. She swept the other faces with a quick glance that halted at a pair of bright, quizzical eyes. Only one man had apparently understood the meaning of her racket at the stove.

"That bum!" said Jac, and turned on her heel.

But something made her stop and look back. Perhaps it was the brightness of those eyes; certainly nothing else could have made her look twice at this fellow. Even among these rough citizens of the mountain desert he was wild and ragged. His shirt was soiled and frayed from elbow to wrist. A bush of black hair was so long that it almost entirely hid his ears, and his face, apparently untouched by a razor for months, was covered by a tremendous growth of whiskers. She could only faintly guess at the features behind that mask.

It was very puzzling, but Jac would not waste time thinking of such a caricature of a man as he of the many whiskers. She turned back into the kitchen and broke off her meditations by kicking a box across the floor.

It smashed against the wall. Jac sat down to think, and stared gloomily straight before her. Her throat swelled and in her heart was that feeling of infinite age which comes upon women at all periods of their life, but most of all during the interim when a girl knows that she is mature and the rest of the world has not yet found it out.

"Why was I made like this?" said Jac miserably.

And from within a still, small voice that was **not** conscience answered her.

"Aw," said the voice, "quit kiddin' yourself!"

"Why," repeated Jac dolorously, "was I tied to such a face?"

"You might as well be askin'," said the voice, "how the colors are painted on a pinto."

"Them colors never rub out."

"Neither will your face."

"It's awful."

"It is."

She stood in front of the speckled mirror.

"There's something wrong with the way I fix my hair," she muttered.

It was tied so tightly that it pulled up the skin of her forehead and raised her eyebrows to a look of continual plaintiveness.

"There's *certainly* something wrong with the way I do my hair!"

"Is that all that's wrong with your face?" whispered the voice.

"My hair is red," said Jac.

"Like paint," said the voice.

"There's no help?"

"None!"

To escape from this merciless dialogue, Jac went back to her post of vantage. The square shoulders of Maurie Gordon were just disappearing through the outer door. All the others were gone, with the exception of her father, her brother Harry, and the man of many whiskers. The last was hardly to be considered as a human being. She felt practically alone with her family, so she entered the dining-room and sat on the edge of the table swinging her feet.

"Harry," she said, "d'you see anything the matter with the way I fix my hair?" Her brother glanced at her with unseeing eyes. The man of many whiskers stopped stirring his coffee and glanced up with the keen twinkle which Jac had seen before. She turned her shoulder upon him.

"Throw me your tobacco, pa," said Harry.

"Did you hear me ask you a question?" said Jac fiercely.

Harry rolled his cigarette before he answered.

"Don't get so sore you rope an' tie yourself. What did you say?"

"I asked you if you was goin' to the dance at Bridewell."

The stranger chuckled softly.

"Say, what's eatin' you, Whiskers?" snapped Jac, but without turning.

"Sure I'm going," said Harry. "It's going to be a big bust."

"What girl are you takin'?"

"Nobody. I'll find plenty to dance with when I get there."

Jac blinked her eyes once, twice, and again.

"Why not take me?"

The cigarette fell from Harry's lips.

"What the—" he began. "Say, Jac, are you sick?"

The ache came in Jac's throat again. Her face changed color and the freckles across the bridge of her nose stood out with a startling distinctness.

"Don't I dance good enough, Harry?" He had evidently been bracing himself for a straight-from-the-shoulder retort. At this gentle question he gasped and rose with a look of brotherly concern.

"Jac, if you was a man I'd say you'd been hittin' the red-eye too much."

"Oh," said Jac.

Harry touched her under the chin and tilted back her head. The deep-blue eyes stared miserably up to him.

"What's the matter with her, pa?" he asked.

"Plain foolishness!" said the latter.

Jac struck the hand from her chin and leaped from the table to her feet.

"Harry," she said, "if I was a man I'd hang a bunch of fives on your chin!"

The chuckle of the stranger made her whirl.

"Get out, Whiskers," she commanded, "or I'll pull a gun an' give you a free shave."

The man rose obediently and went from the room to the porch. Harry followed him out and swung into the saddle of his horse. His father delayed an instant.

"Now cut out this talk of goin' to the dance," said Jim During. "You stay right here, an' if any of the boys come in late fix them up some chow. I got to slide over to see old Jones on some—some business."

  A SAGEBRUSH CINDERELLA

"Sure you do," said Jac scornfully. "I know that kind of business. It comes five in a hand and you draw to it."

The hair of her father seemed to take on a deeper tinge of red.

"Well?" he said.

"Well?" she replied no less angrily. "If I couldn't play no better hand of poker than you do, I'd go no farther than solitaire, believe me."

"Jacqueline!"

"Don't swear at me!" said Jac. "If you think I ain't right, just sit down and play a hand with me."

Her father was so swelled with wrath that he could make no rejoinder. At length he whirled on his heel and strode toward the door, pulling his sombrero down over his eyes.

At the door he turned back and pointed a long, angry arm.

"An' if I catch you leavin' this place to-night—" he began.

"Well?"

His face altered and the anger faded from his eyes.

"Jac," he said gently, "why in hell wasn't you born a boy?"

He went on out and a moment later his horse clattered down the road.

"Why?" repeated Jac.

CHAPTER II

LAND

She went out to the porch and stared after the disappearing horseman. When he had quite vanished in the rapidly fading light of the evening she turned back. She stopped. The stranger sat on the edge of the porch whittling a stick.

His black hair bushed out under the brim of his sombrero, and for some reason it stirred the latent wrath in Jac. She went to him and stood with arms akimbo, staring down.

"Too bad," he said, but did not look up.

"What's too bad?"

"The red hair."

It was a long moment before she spoke. "Huh!" she said. "If I was to talk about *your* hair you'd think I was discussin' a record crop of hay. If I was to—"

She stopped, for the twinkling eyes were smiling up to her.

"I look like the land of much rain, all right," said the stranger.

Jac dropped to a cross-legged position with the agility of an Indian and supporting her chin on both hands she stared impudently into the face of the stranger.

"What does the land look like when the forest is gone?"

"It ain't been surveyed for so long I've forgotten."

He shifted a little to smile more directly into her eyes, and the movement caused her glance to drop to his holster. It was open. With a slow gesture—for no one, not even a woman, makes free with the weapon of another in the mountain desert—she drew the revolver out, looked it over with the keen eye of a connoisseur, glanced down the sights, spun the cylinder, and tried the balance with a deft hand.

"Clean as a whistle," she said as she restored the revolver. "**Some** six-gun!" With a new respect she looked the man over from head to foot.

"Maybe under the mask," she said, "you look almost human."

"I dunno. Maybe."

Her eyes wandered far away; came back to him, frowned; wandered off again.

"Can you dance?" she asked conversationally.

He broke into a deep laughter. Jac gathered as if for a spring.

"Go slow, partner," she drawled. "Maybe I ain't big, but believe me, I ain't a house pet."

"I'd as soon think of fondlin' a wildcat," nodded the man.

She hesitated between anger and curiosity, and then glanced around with needless anxiety lest they should not be alone.

"Give it to me straight, pal," she said. "How bad do I look?"

Her companion looked her over with a critical eye and a judicious frown.

"I dunno," he said at last. "It's pretty hard for me to tell. If those freckles was covered up, maybe I could see your face." As he spoke he edged away, as if ready to spring from the porch when she attacked him.

Instead, she sighed. The other started and looked at her with a new interest.

"How old are you?" he asked sharply.

"Three years more than you think."

"Sixteen?"

"And three makes nineteen. You're right the first time. How'd you do it?"

He took off his hat and extended his hand.

"My name is Bill Carrigan," he said.

Even in the dim light he could guess at the curiosity in her eyes.

"Mine is Jac—Jacqueline During. I'm awfully glad to shake hands with you."

There was a little pause.

"I suppose Maurie Gordon is nearly at the dance by this time?" he said tentatively.

She nodded. The lump in her throat kept her silent.

"How tall are you?" he asked suddenly.

"Five feet five and a half."

"What's your weight?"

"One hundred and twenty. Say, Carrigan, what you drivin' at?"

He looked away as if making a mental note.

"What size shoes?"

She looked at him with a dark frown, but the twinkle of his eyes was irresistible. She broke into a laugh.

"Look at 'em!"

She extended to his gaze a foot clad in the heavy shoe of a man, cut square across the toe.

"Well, Columbus, what have you discovered?"

"Land," said Carrigan, and rose.

"You goin' so soon?" she queried plaintively.

"But I'm coming back," said Carrigan.

"Coming back?" repeated Jac.

"With bells."

She watched him swing gracefully into the saddle of a clean-limbed horse and gallop swiftly into the gloom.

"Well, I'll be—" began Jac.

She checked herself. An instinct which was born with Eve made her raise a hand to pat her hair.

She began again: "I must look like—" Once more she stopped, this time with a sigh. "What words are left?" murmured Jacqueline.

Carrigan pulled his horse up before the barber shop in the little village a mile away. He banged thunderously against the wall of the shanty with his gun-butt.

"What the hell!" roared a voice above.

"Business," said Carrigan. "Come on down and open your shop."

A few moments later he sat down in the chair while the barber lighted his lamp. The latter groaned when he saw the face of his customer.

"How much?"

"The price of your best razor," said Carrigan instantly. "Now start— chop off the heavy timber, saw down the undergrowth, anything to clear the land. And do it on the jump."

Hair flew—literally. At last the barber stepped back, perspiring, and looked at the lean face before him.

"I feel," he said, "more as if I'd made a man than shaved him."

"Maybe you're right," said Carrigan, and started on the run for the general merchandise store across the street, the only clothiers within a hundred miles, a place that carried everything from horseshoes to hairpins. The proprietor was locking up the front door.

"What's your rush, partner?" he asked. "Wait till to-morrow. I got some business to—"

"To-morrow is next year," said Carrigan. "Start goin'."

The door opened.

He began shedding orders and old clothes at the same time. The storekeeper, on the run, brought the articles Carrigan demanded.

"More light!" Carrigan said at last.

The proprietor brought a lamp and placed it close to a large mirror, the pride of his place.

Carrigan stalked up to it, and, turning slowly around, viewed his outfit with one long glance.

"All right," he said. "Now I'm ready to begin buying!"

The proprietor gasped and then rubbed his hands.

"What next?" he asked.

"A beautiful girl."

The proprietor smiled in sympathy with the somewhat obscure jest.

"A beautiful girl," repeated Carrigan, "with red hair, weighing a trifle over one hundred and twenty pounds, standing five feet five and a half, and with feet—well, of the right size."

The proprietor moistened his lips and stepped back. His eyes were very large.

"Start for the ladies' department."

The proprietor was baffled, but he led the way.

"Dresses first," said Carrigan. "Some thing fancy. Best you've got. Here! Red—green! green—red!"

He picked out a gown and held it out at arm's length, a soft, green fabric.

"What size do you want?" asked the proprietor.

"What's the perfect size for five foot five, eh?"

"Thirty-six."

"What's this gown?"

"Thirty-six."

"How much?"

The proprietor doubled the price.

"Taken," said Carrigan.

"But maybe the lady ain't thirty-six, and—"

"You're right, old-timer. The lady ain't, but she will be. What's next? Petticoat?"

"Those are over here."

"I leave it to you, partner. Something that makes a rustle and a swishing like a light rain on leaves. You know the kind?"

"Taffeta will do that."

"Then taffeta it is. Now for the kicks. Something light. Slippers, eh?"

"Follow me."

He set out an array of dancing-shoes.

"What size?" he asked.

"The right size."

The proprietor made a gesture of despair.

"There ain't no woman in the world whose feet are the **right** size."

"Then we'll set a record to-night. How big ought they to be for a hundred and twenty pounds?"

"That all depends. If the lady is—"

"The lady ain't," repeated Carrigan wearily. "I'm tellin' you we're making her here."

The proprietor wiped his forehead.

"Number four?" he suggested vaguely. "Let's have a look. Make it something like this."

He indicated a pair of bronze slippers, but when the storekeeper produced the pair of number fours, Carrigan took one of them in the palm of his brawny hand and stared at it with something between awe and dismay.

"Are these meant for real feet?"

"Yep."

Carrigan thought of the mighty brogans he had seen on Jac's feet.

"Do or die," he said, "she'll have to wear 'em! What's next? Stockings?"

"Here they are."

"These green ones will do the work. And now—"

"Corsets?"

He indicated a model bust clad in a formidable corset.

Carrigan sighed.

"Friend," he said, "did you ever hear about the days when men wore armor?"

"Yes."

"When I'm dancin' with a girl that wears one of them things, I feel as if I had my arms around a man in armor. Anything else?"

A malicious light gleamed in the eyes of the proprietor.

"There's nothing else except these girdles that a drummer palmed off on me. They're jest elastic, that's all. They don't give a girl no figger."

"H-m! But they're a long way from armor-plate. I'll take one."

"What size?"

"How do they run? Large, small, and medium?"

"By inches."

"Make it something extra medium in inches."

"Most of 'em **wish** they could wear twenty-one."

"Twenty-one it is."

The proprietor grinned.

"But if that's too small—"

"Friend, what do you do when your cinch is too small for your hoss?"

"Pull."

"Well?"

The proprietor added the girdle to the heap in mute surrender.

"And now that we've got down to the girdle," he said, "the next thing is—"

"Look here, friend," said Carrigan, "don't go too far!"

"Well?"

"Well, fix up the underlining any way you want, but make it the best you've got. One thing more. There ain't enough color in this outfit. Something for her shoulders?"

"A scarf. Right here."

Carrigan picked out a filmy, orchid-colored tissue.

"Now we've reached her face."

The proprietor groaned.

"Paint?"

"Nope. I don't want to add anything. I want to make something disappear. Freckles."

The storekeeper grinned.

"Vanishing cream and then rice powder. That's the latest hitch."

CHAPTER III

CINDERELLA

The bundle which resulted was bulky, but Carrigan sang as he raced back. He drew his horse to a walk as he approached the During hotel, for a light showed dimly from the dining-room; there might be some new arrival in the place.

It was only Jac, however. She sat by the table with her face buried in her arms. He saw one hand lying palm up beside her head. It was small and the fingers tapered.

"I never noticed she was so small," said Carrigan to himself in a hushed voice.

He stepped closer, softly.

"Jest a kid," he added.

There was the sound of a controlled sob; her body quivered; and Carrigan knew that she was struggling with some great grief.

"Cinderella!" he called gently and touched her shoulder.

Her head turned. Two marvelously deep-blue eyes shone up to him. Her lower lip was trembling; but when she saw him she stiffened with astonishment.

"What do you want?" she asked.

"A beautiful girl, five feet five and a half, one hundred and twenty pounds."

"Carrigan!" she stammered. "Is it really you?"

He dropped the bundle to the floor and turned slowly.

"Look me over."

"Wonderful!"

She had dropped into a chair and sat pigeon-toed, her hands clasped tightly in her lap and her mouth slightly agape.

"Carrigan, how did you do it?"

"Look in that bundle and you'll see." He left the room hastily, but before he had gone far he heard a thin, short cry. Happiness and pain are closely akin.

"If she only—" began Carrigan.

He choked.

"If this was only a masked ball," he said at last, "she might get by. But even then that hair—"

He swore softly again.

"If Maurie turns her down after this—I'll bust his face wide open."

He thought of Gordon's wide shoulders and sighed.

After a time a voice called from the house:

"Carrigan!"

It was a marvelous voice. It was changed as the tone of a violin changes when it passes from the hands of an amateur to those of an artist.

"Is that my name?" said Carrigan, and he walked slowly toward the house.

She stood in the center of the room, with a piece of the wrapping-paper in which the bundle had been done up held before her face.

Carrigan started back until his shoulders touched the wall.

"My God!" he murmured with indescribable awe. "They fit!"

"But—" she said behind the paper.

"Well?"

She lowered the paper. The freckles looked out at him—and the eyes with plaintive brows raised by the hard knot of the hair. At the base of her throat was a line of sharp division. All above was a healthy brown. All below was a dazzling white.

He could not meet the despair of her eyes.

"Well?" she said.

"Well?" said Carrigan.

"I didn't choose this face," she explained sadly. "It was wished on me!"

Carrigan sank into a chair and looked upon her as a general looks over a field of battle and calculates the chances of his outnumbered army. His eyes fell to the slender feet in the shining bronze slippers, with the small, round ankles incased in pleasant green.

His heart leaped. His eyes raised and met the freckles. He clenched his hand.

"If it wasn't for them freckles—"

"Yes?"

"I could see your face."

Crimson went up her throat with delicate tints, blending the clear white of the breast with the brown of the round neck. He jumped to his feet: he pointed a commanding arm.

"That hair!"

"I know it's—"

"I don't care what you know. Untie that knot!"

She obeyed. A red gold flood rippled suddenly almost to her knees.

Carrigan blinked.

"Sit down!"

She dropped to a chair, and Carrigan commenced to work. When a man has to do anything from roping a steer to jerking out a six-gun with the speed of light, he acquires a marvelous dexterity with his hands. Carrigan could almost think with his fingers. They seemed, in fact, to have a separate intelligence.

He gathered up the silken mass. The soft touch thrilled him as if every one of the delicate threads carried a tiny charge of electricity. It was marvelous that such a shining torrent could have been reduced the moment before to that compacted, bright red knot.

Carrigan closed his eyes and summoned up a vision of hair as he had seen it dressed, not on the heads of any of the mountain-desert belles, but in magazine pictures.

With that vision before him he commenced to work, rapidly, surely. It seemed as if the hair, glad to escape from the bondage of that hard knot, fell of its own accord into graceful, waving lines. It curved low across the broad forehead: it gathered at the nape of the neck in a soft knot in the Grecian mode.

"Now!" said Carrigan.

She rose and faced him.

"What's happened?" she cried, for his lower jaw had fallen.

He swallowed twice before he could answer.

"I'm beginning to see your face!"

For the face, after all, is like any picture. The hair is the frame, and an ugly frame will spoil the most lovely painting. The eye does not stop at a boundary. It includes it.

"Once more!" said Carrigan, and seized the vanishing cream.

As he worked now he felt like the artist who draws the human face from the block of marble. He felt as Michelangelo when the grim old Florentine said: "I do not create; I take off the outer layers of the stone and free the form which is hidden within." Or perhaps he was more like Pygmalion and the inevitable statue when the artist saw the first hues of life faintly flushing in the cold marble.

When he stepped back and looked at her, she seemed strangely aloof. She had drawn away a thousand miles and a thousand years. He discovered the most ancient of truths, that a beautiful woman is a world in herself upon which all men must look from the outside. She escapes from experience. It cannot stain her. She escapes from herself. Her beauty is greater than her soul.

"It's done," said Carrigan sadly.

"Isn't it any use?" she queried.

He thought of Maurie and hated the handsome face which rose in his memory.

"You look sick," said Jac. "What's the matter? Is it all in my face? Let me take a slant at the landscape after the snow has fallen."

She ran to the cracked glass. She was a tomboy when she whirled to a stop in front of it. He watched her eyes widen; saw her straighten slightly, wonderfully. She was inches taller when she turned; she was years older.

"Are you ready, Mr. Carrigan?"

She moved to him with a subtle rustling like the fall of a misting rain on orchard blossoms. He could not answer for a moment. He had seen a miracle.

"Yes, Miss During," he said at last.

The light which came somewhere from the depths to shine in her eyes altered swiftly to a sparkle which he could understand.

She ran to him and caught both his hands.

"Carrigan," said Jac, "you're a trump!"

"And you," said he, "are the ace of the suit. Let's go!"

"One thing first," she said, and ran into another room.

She came back almost at once with a chain of amber beads about her throat—a loop of golden fire, trembling and changing with every breath she drew. She slipped the orchid-colored scarf over her shoulders. It was like a mist tinged by the dainty light of dawn. Three times the rich color was repeated; first in the red gold glory of her hair, then in the flash of fire that looped her throat, and last it splashed across the bronze slippers. But with the orchid-colored scarf the charm was complete; the spell was cast.

"How are we to go?" she asked as they stood beside his horse.

He looked on her with some doubt. The dim light caught at the amber beads.

"Perhaps we'll have to ride double," he ventured.

Her laughter reassured him. She caught the pommel of the saddle as if to vault up, man-fashion. Then she remembered, with a murmur of dismay.

"How—" she began.

He caught her beneath the arms and lifted her lightly to the saddle, then sprang up behind. The horse started at a slow trot.

"Carrigan?"

"Well?"

"Harry is at the dance. If he should recognize me?"

"He won't."

She chuckled. There was a brooding mischief in the tone that set him tingling.

"Are you sure?"

"Did the people recognize Cinderella at the ball?"

"And if there should be trouble because I'm recognized?"

"This fairy godmother wears a six-gun."

They were silent a moment.

"How far is it to Bridewell?" he asked at last.

"Eight miles—by the road."

"We're late already. Is there any short cut?"

"Across the river it's between two and three."

"The river?"

"It ain't very deep—sometimes. I've done it, but never in duds like these."

"Are you game to try the short cut across the river?"

Her head tilted back as she laughed. That was her answer. It was not laughter. It was music. It was the singing of one whose dreams are coming true, and where it left off on her lips the sound was continued like a silent echo in Carrigan.

As she swung the horse to the left toward the ford of the river, a puff of warm wind floated the scarf against Carrigan's face. He could scarcely feel its gossamer web, but a faint fragrance came from it, and his heart beat fast. The moon rolled like a yellow wheel over the tops of the black hills, and its light touched the throat and the turned face of Jacqueline, so that Carrigan could barely guess at her smile. When he spoke to her she did not turn. She stared straight before, crooning a hushed, joyous melody deep in her throat.

She would not turn her head, for then the vision with which she rode would have vanished. While she looked straight before her past the tossing head of the horse, it was not Carrigan who sat at her shoulder; it was not his voice which spoke to her; it was not his breath which touched her throat now and again. No! For though the horse had not journeyed far, Jacqueline had ridden a fabulous distance into the regions of romance. The amber beads were now a chain of gold, and where they touched cold against her breast, that was where the jeweled cross lay, the priceless relic before which she said her prayers at dawn and evening. The hair was no longer red. It was yellower, richer than that golden moon. The slight clinking of the bridle-rein, where the little chain chimed against the bit, that was the rattle of the armor of her knight. He had ridden far for her that evening. He had stolen into the castle of her father. He had reached her chamber, where the tapestries made a hushing along the wall like warning whispers. And he had lowered her from the casement on a rope made of twisted clothes. And he had helped her across the moat. Then, with a rusted key, they turned the harsh lock of a secret portal and were free—free—free!

Jacqueline tossed up her arms. The air was like a cool caress upon them. Yes, she was free! They topped a hill. Below it ran the river, glimmering silver through the night, and jeweled by the shining of the stars. Suddenly she shook the reins and urged the horse to a frantic gallop down the slope.

"What's the matter?" cried Carrigan.

Yes, how could he know that even at that moment her father, with a band of hard-riding liegemen, had thundered into view behind them and that death raced closely on their heels? She drew rein, panting on the edge of the river.

Then Carrigan proved himself a knight indeed. They dared not imperil that gown of green, so he sat in the saddle with his legs crossed in front of the horn and lifted her in his arms. Then he gave the horse its way, and the cunning old cattle-pony picked a safe way along a sand-bank. The water rose higher. They slipped, floundering into little hollows, and clambered back into shallower places. Once the water rose so high that Carrigan could have put down his hand and touched it.

"Steady!" he said encouragingly to the girl.

The voice was deep and vibrant. It blended with her dream of romance. Her tyrant father with his villain knights sat their horses on the bank of the river, not daring to attempt the passage, and now that her hero was about to bear her safe to the other shore— She drew a long breath and relaxed in his arms, her strong, young body now soft and yielding. The horse pawed for a footing and then lurched up the bank with a snort. Her arms tightened around Carrigan's neck; her lips pressed eagerly to his.

"Jac!"

How could he know that that word carried her dream away like dead leaves on a wind? She covered her face from him.

"We are late already," she said.

CHAPTER IV

THE SONG OF SONGS

The dance-hall was the up-stairs floor of Bridewell's general merchandise store. From the center of the ceiling was suspended a monstrous gasoline-lamp that flooded the larger part of the dancing floor with dazzling light, but the flicker of the flame sent occasional seas of shadow washing into the corners of the room. A thick line of stools and chairs and empty grocery-boxes made the seats for the throng around the wall. The floor glimmered and shone in mute testimony to the polishing which it had received earlier in the evening when a dozen strong men pulled about the room a heavy bale of hay with two men sitting upon it. Waxed hardwood could not have been more brilliant.

The music was supplied by a banjo, a slide trombone, a violin, and a snare drum; and the musicians operated their instruments with undying vigor. Lest they should falter in their efforts from weariness, glasses of liquor stood beside them at all times, supplied by generous cow-punchers who appreciated the soulful music. This stimulus was not applied in vain, for, as the evening wore on, each piece of music was increased slightly but perceptibly in cadence beyond all which had gone before.

This applied to the two-steps, which sent the dancers whirling over the floor with such violence that at the end of each dance there was a general stampede for the bar which stretched across the farther end of the room. Here four men worked with frantic haste to quench the thirst of the multitude, and labored in vain. The exercise made the throat of every man as dry as that of Tantalus, and the glasses were snatched up and tossed off as rapidly as they were spun down the length of the bar.

Jac and Carrigan paused at the door to make a survey of the scene. The festivities were already well under way. Some of the men had removed their bandannas and stuffed the latter into back trouser-pockets, from which they streamed like brilliant pennons during the dance. There were other tokens that the dance had passed the stiff formality of the opening moments. The musicians played with the fierce resolution of long-distance runners entering the homestretch. The violinist leaned back with eyes closed and jaw set in do-or-die determination, while his bow darted back and forth across the strings. The banjo man leaned far over and thrummed away with an expression partly of pain and partly of faraway yearning as he stared above the heads of the dancers. The expression was caused not by sorrow of soul, but by a cramp in his right hand. The trombone-player, however, was in far worse case than either of his two companions. He was very fat, very short, and his red, bald head shone furiously. Yet he would not diminish the vigor of his efforts. His long slurs were more brazenly ringing than ever. His upward runs raised the heart and the hair at the same time. His downward slides sent out a chill tingle along the spine. He jerked out his arm with such violence that it made his flabby body quiver like jelly; and the vigor of his blowing set a white spot in the middle of his puffed cheeks.

Orpheus stirred the trees as this orchestra stirred the citizens of the mountain-desert. It sent them whirling frantically about the dance-hall; it moved them to sit now and then in the shadow-swept corners, closely tête-à-tête.

A wild and ludicrous scene? Perhaps. But also there was beauty and youth as much as ever graced a ballroom. And there was rhythm. Rhythm of the dance, rhythm of the screeching, thrumming music; and to the young, rhythm is poetry. It set a glamour upon the faces of the dancers; of the shadowy corners it made moonlit gardens.

　　　　　　　　　　　　　　　A SAGEBRUSH CINDERELLA

"What is my name?" queried Jac. "We forgot that!"

He was dumfounded.

"Perhaps I'm your sister?"

He grinned.

"Jac, you look as much like me as a yearling short-horn looks like a long-horn maverick. Something fancy. Jacqueline Silvestre. How does that hit, eh? Miss Silvestre! You've come from the east. You're visiting at a ranch twenty miles away."

"What ranch?"

"Fake a name."

"Every one knows everybody else for miles around."

"It's up to you. Can you do the Eastern lingo?"

She tilted her head to one side and gazed upon him with naive astonishment.

"'Lingo,' Mr. Carrigan?"

"Good Lord!" breathed Carrigan.

Her laughter was low and filled with hints of many things. It made him distinctly uncomfortable.

"I've read books," she said. "I'll do my part. But you?"

"I'm simply a cow-puncher you've pressed into service to bring you here. Right? Now who do you want to dance with? Watch their eyes!"

They walked slowly into the room, and were met by a new sound over the clangor of music and voices. It was that buzz which to the heart of the debutante is the elixir of life, and to the city matron is the nectar which promises immortal beauty. In the dance-hall at Bridewell it was less covert. Jacqueline stood in the spot-light like a queen.

She knew that her color had heightened. She knew that the flare of the gasoline-lamp made her hair a glorious dull-red fire, touched with golden points of light, which fell again on the necklace at her throat, the only heirloom she had received from her mother, and still further down on the bronze slippers. The admiration of the men filled her heart; the trouble in the more covert stares of the girls overflowed it. A sense of power flooded in her like electricity. She knew that when she turned and dropped her hand on the arm of Carrigan it sent a tingle through him.

Her smile was casual and her eyes calm. Her whisper was surcharged with a vital anxiety.

"Do you dance—well?"

"Regular fairy," grinned Carrigan, and she wished his mouth was not so broad. "How about you?"

"Not so bad."

"Let's start."

Dancers are not made even by infinite pains and lessons. They are born, and Jac was a born dancer. With the smooth floor underfoot, the light slippers, the pulse and urge of the music, however crude, the newborn sense of dignity and womanly power, she became an artist. She danced not to the music, but to what the music might have been.

Through the film of pleasure she vaguely knew that people were giving way a little before her. She knew the eyes of the girls were upon her feet. She knew the eyes of the men were upon her face and the sway of the graceful body, and among those eyes she found one pair more bright and devouring than all the rest. It was Maurie Gordon.

He was dancing with a little golden-haired beauty, Dolly Maxwell. She let her eyes rest carelessly upon him. She smiled. Handsome Maurie started as though some one had stepped on his foot. He stumbled—he lost his step—his little partner frowned up at him and then flashed a look of utter hate toward Jac. A girl may guess at the heart of a man, but she can absolutely read the soul of another woman. It is a subtle system of wireless which tells a thousand words in a single smile; a glance is a spark driven by ten thousand volts. The heart of Jacqueline swelled with the Song of Songs.

"Do something!" she murmured in the ear of Carrigan.

He met her eyes with a cold understanding.

"You've just seen Maurie Gordon?" he asked.

"You're dancing wonderfully," she pleaded, "but do something new."

"Do you know the Carrigan cut?"

"I'll try it."

"It's a cross between a glide, a dip, and a roll. Take three short steps, then take a long, draggy slide to the left—and let yourself go."

The trombone started an upward flourish. They followed it, running forward. She began the draggy step to the left—and then let herself go. How it was done, she could not tell, but somehow he took her weight in the middle of the step, and they completed a little dipping whirl as graceful as the lilt of a seagull against a flurry of wind.

A gasp of applause broke out around them. The dancers veered further off to allow room for these beautiful new maneuvers. And Jacqueline, dizzy with the joy of conquest, saw the set, white face of Dolly Maxwell. It was the golden drop of honey in the wine of victory. The music stopped, but the rhythm still ran in her blood.

Carrigan's rather coldly curious stare sobered her.

"What's the matter?" she asked.

"I see a freckle comin' out to look the landscape over. Sorry you ain't got that powder-puff with you."

"I have it, all right."

"I didn't know you had pockets in that dress."

"It's my corsage."

"Your which?"

"Look at that funny trombone-player." He turned to stare at the shiny bald head, and when he looked back she had just slipped something into the bosom of her dress. All traces of the freckle were gone. She flushed a little under his eye of inquiry. Then very anxiously: "Is it gone?"

"It's behind a cloud, anyway," said Carrigan. "Here's Maurie Gordon."

The big cow-puncher came up, earnest-eyed.

"If you're not hooked up for this next waltz—" he began.

He stopped with a widening stare. She had glanced carelessly over him from head to foot, and now turned her back on him to take the arm of Carrigan. The movement was slow, deliberate, casual. It left big Maurie Gordon crimson and breathing hard, the butt of open laughter from all.

A SAGEBRUSH CINDERELLA

CHAPTER V

THE SILVESTRE SLIDE

Carrigan found Jac trembling with excitement, though her face was still calm.

"What the devil," he began. "I thought Gordon was the man you wanted—"

"Don't you get me?" she broke in eagerly. "None of those swell Eastern ladies would bat an eye at a bum who came up to them without bein' introduced."

"Oh!" said Carrigan. "And who—"

"You will," she answered without hesitation. "Take me over to a chair and talk with me a minute. Then you can sidestep up to the bar and get a drink. When all the boys flock around and ask about me—"

He growled: "How do you know they'll flock around and ask about you?"

There was something akin to pity in her smile. The statue was walking away from Pygmalion.

"Take it from me. They will. Your money ain't any good at that bar—take me to that chair standing away from the rest of them—because every man will be wantin' to make your acquaintance an' buy you liquor. Drink beer, Carrie. I hate a breath. Then they'll ask about me, an' you tell 'em that I'm straight from the East, an' don't understand Western ways. Tell 'em they'll have to be introduced. An' don't bring over any one I don't point out."

"Beginnin' with Gordon?"

"Sure. Bring him first."

"Who's next? Are you goin' to corral 'em all?"

"If I want to."

They sat down—Carrigan rather gingerly, and edging away from her.

"You see that skinny feller with the black hair?"

"Yep."

"That's Dave Carey. He's engaged to that girl with the smile an' the fluffy pink dress. She called me a 'horrible tomboy' once. You can bring Dave Carey next."

"Goin' to bust up the happy homes, Jac?"

"Miss Silvestre," she corrected. "Watch Jenny Hendrix stare at me! She's whispering, too. I hate her! Then there's Ben Craig, the tall man with the thin, sad-lookin' face. Once when he was at the hotel he said my head was more like a turkey-egg than a face. You c'n bring him third. I'll think of some more after a while."

"How're you goin' to keep up the bluff with all those fellers? They'll spot your lingo in a minute."

Jacqueline waved the suggestion airily away.

"I read a book once," she said, and her smile was very close to the grin of Jac During, now no more. "It told about an Eastern girl who came West an' she was terrible thrilled about the Western men. She had a great lingo. I'll stick by what she said."

"What was it?"

"Mr. Carrigan, have you lived all your life in the West?"

"Sure."

He started and stared at her.

"Is that part of the lingo?"

"I knew you had been all your life out here in these big open spaces. It makes you so much more real than the Eastern men."

"Huh!" grunted Carrigan, and blinked rapidly.

"Do you know that I feel that you—but you would think me foolish if I said it."

"You bet your life I wouldn't!" gasped Carrigan.

She leaned closer and dropped a hand on his arm. Her gaze dwelt tenderly on his startled eyes.

"I feel that you are the first **real** man I have ever known, Mr. Carrigan."

"The devil you do!"

"Yes. All the men I have met have been so superficial. But you are like your own great West, Mr. Carrigan, with a heart as wide as the desert and as open as the sky. I feel it. Am I foolish to tell you this?"

Carrigan loosened his bandanna.

"Jac, are you goin' to pull this sort of a line on all the boys?" he asked hoarsely.

"Sure I am. Why not? Don't it get by?"

"There'll be gun-play before the night's over, you c'n lay that ten to one."

"Why?"

"Don't look at me like that! You make me nervous. It ain't what you say so much as the way you say it. Where'd you learn that way of talkin'?"

"I been to the movies, an' I used my eyes. I've seen Maude Merriam an' come home an' practised at the mirror. Has she got anything on me?"

"She generally ain't got half so much on," groaned Carrigan, and rose.

"Wait a minute, Carrie!"

"Say, Cinderella, maybe I'm the fairy godmother, but don't go callin' me by a woman's name. The brand don't no ways look well on my hide."

"All right, Mr. Carrigan. But just remember this: That ain't the Carrigan cut that we done in the last dance."

He rubbed a hand across his forehead.

"It's the Silvestre slide."

"What?"

"Sure. I introduced it in New York, an' everybody in the Five Hundred copied it an' named it after me. It made an awful hit."

Carrigan fled. He went straight for the bar by instinct, for he began to need a drink. Jacqueline proved a prophet. As he dropped his coin on the bar a broad hand swept it back to him. He looked up into the handsome, serious face of Maurie Gordon.

"Partner," said Maurie, "this drink's on me. My name's Gordon."

"Wait a minute, Maurie," broke in another voice. "You're lickerin' with me, friend. I'm Dave Carey. Glad to meet you. Two comin' up, bartender!"

"I'm drinkin' beer," said Carrigan, remembering orders.

An odd look, which he understood perfectly, came in the eyes of the other men.

"Look here," went on Maurie, "that girl you brung to the dance is a hell bender. If you ain't dancin' all evenin' with her, maybe I could break in, eh?"

He reinforced his suggestion with a broad wink and a tremendous slap on the shoulder.

"Maybe you could," said Carrigan.

"I'll have to introduce you. Miss Silvestre is straight from the East, an' she don't quite get the hang of our Western ways."

"Straight from the East?"

"Yep. New York, an' all that. Blood as blue as hell."

"The devil!"

"It is, all right, till you get to know her."

"How'd you pick her up?"

"She's been visitin' at the ranch where I work. We sort of ran off together tonight. She was strong for some sort of a lark. Kind of nifty?"

"*Is* she?"

"But you got to talk careful to her, get me?"

"I'll hang on to my tongue like it was a buckin' bronco."

"Then foller me."

"Hold on," said Carey desperately. "Carrigan, don't I get no look in here?"

"What d'you want to go hangin' around with every girl in the country for?" queried Gordon, and his frown was dangerous. "Ain't you engaged already?"

"Am I?" replied Carey, with an ominous lowering of the voice. "An' ain't Dolly Maxwell got you roped and throwed?"

"Suppose," broke in Carrigan anxiously, "that you get introduced at the same time, an' then Gordon c'n have the first dance an' you get the next."

They compromised on this basis and trooped obediently behind Carrigan.

"Wait a minute," said Gordon. "Maybe you'd like to meet Dolly Maxwell?"

"Sure," said Carrigan.

They stopped before the girl of the golden hair. There was soul-deep understanding in the cold eye she fixed upon Maurie Gordon. Carrigan received gushing recognition, not for him, he knew, but for the partner of the sensation in green.

"The next dance? Sure you can have it. Good-by, Maurie."

But her parting shot was wasted on thin air. Maurie was headed for other and more pleasant regions, and the light of the discoverer was in his eye. He was a new Balboa looking out upon another Pacific. They ranged before Jac.

"Miss Silvestre, this is Mr. Gordon, an' Mr. Carey."

Maurie searched his memory, steeled his nerves, and spoke: "I sure feel it's a privilege to know you."

"Me, too," said Carey, and then bit his lips.

The scorn of a superior intelligence was haughty in the face of big Maurie.

"Thank you," Jac was saying. "Will you sit down?"

"Sure," said Maurie, and plumped into the chair beside her. "Maybe you ain't got the next dance taken. Can I have it? Thanks."

He glared his triumph at Carey, who turned away, dark-eyed with envy.

The cold glance of Jac cut short Carrigan's incipient grin.

"So-long," he said, and turned on his heel.

He joined Dave Carey.

"Fourteen degrees of frost in her smile," said that worthy, "but I'm bettin' on a river runnin' under the ice."

"Are you goin' to dance?"

"Nope. I need a drink. Have one on me?"

"I got work ahead," said Carrigan, and made for Dolly Maxwell.

CHAPTER VI

THE GIRL FROM FIFTH AVENUE

"'So long,'" quoted Jac. "Is that the Western way of saving good-by, Mr. Gordon?"

There was a serious question in her eyes. Maurie leaned back and drew a deep breath.

"Maybe your friend Carrigan talks that way, an' I've heard some others say the same thing, but it ain't considered partic'lar choice. Most of us says 'adios' or something like that."

"Oh, I thought it was rather queer, but then Mr. Carrigan is"—she paused—"rather queer in lots of ways!"

It was plain that she considered him different. The music began. They danced. The rather diffident arm of big Maurie gathered strength and confidence.

"You sure c'n throw your feet!" he burst out at length.

"You ain't travelin' very far behind," said Jac, amiably.

She felt Maurie start. She knew—with a growing coldness of heart—that he was staring down at her face with question. With a great effort she made her eyes rise and rest artlessly upon his. She was hunting her book-vocabulary desperately.

"I've picked that up from the western vernacular. Mr. Gordon. Does it sound natural?"

"It sure does."

The doubt was gone from his face. The triumph reinforced her smile. Dolly Maxwell sailed by in the arms of Carrigan. They were dancing beautifully.

"Say," said Gordon with sudden anxiety. "What was that funny step you done with Carrigan?"

"That was the Silvestre Slide, as they call it in New York."

"Oh!"

"I invented it and it was picked up all along Fifth Avenue. You've no idea how quickly things spread in New York. They named it after me."

In his awe he almost lost step. She enjoyed his consternation for a moment and then in pity spoke: "Shall we try it?"

"D'you really think I could get away with it?"

"'Get away with it,' Mr. Gordon?"

"I mean, d'you think I could be taught?"

"Oh, yes. It's this way. It's a cinch!—as you say out here in the west!"

They started the maneuver, but Gordon was afflicted with stage fright. He blundered miserably. A snicker sounded about them, and desire for murder flooded the heart of Jacqueline, for Carrigan and Dolly Maxwell had just executed the step perfectly. She set her teeth and drove ahead.

"Mr. Gordon, have you lived all your life in the West?"

"Yep. Every day of it!"

She sighed.

Then: "That is why you are so different. In the East the boys are so—well, so artificial!"

"Huh?" said Maurie vaguely. "That so?"

"But you are like your own wild west! with a heart as big as your mountain-desert and as open as your skies!"

The arm of Maurie tightened. She felt his breath coming quickly against her hair, and she thought of the spilled coffee and the "damnation!" of earlier in that same evening. Life was sweet indeed!

"What makes you so unusual, Mr. Gordon?"

Once, twice her lips stirred before the words came.

"It's a hard life on the range. It takes a strong man to get by."

"You look strong, Mr. Gordon."

Laughter makes the voice purr, and there was a caress in the tone of Jacqueline. He stiffened, throwing his shoulders back.

"In a pinch I've done a man's work," he said modestly.

"I've heard about men who can take a steer by the horns and wrestle until they throw the big animal—but I suppose that is just western joking?"

"Nope. I don't think nothin' at all of throwin' a steer."

"Oh! And aren't you afraid of—of their nasty horns?"

She stammered with admiration and wonder.

"I was brung up to take chances. Throwin' a steer ain't much— for a man like me. You see, I got the size for it. A feller needs weight on the range."

"But some of these cow-punchers seem quite slender."

"Yep. But they don't count much for a real man's work. Take Carrigan, over there. I guess he's a pretty fair sort when it comes to gettin' around, but he ain't got the weight. I guess he weighs about twenty pounds less'n I do."

"Do you know that I feel—but you would think me foolish if I said it!"

"Lady—Miss—Miss Silvestre, you c'n lay ten to one I won't think anything you say is foolish!"

"Well, then, I feel as if you are the only real man I have ever known."

"Honest?" said the deep, quivering voice.

"Yes. The rest I cannot understand. I—I stifle among them!"

"You ain't stringin' me along?"

"What other men say are merely words. But such a man as you are, speaks from the heart. I know! I could believe you!"

"Miss Silvestre—"

"Isn't it usual in the West to be called by first names?"

There was a sound of choking. Her wide, wondering eyes raised to his.

"Or is it wrong, Mr. Gordon? To be called by one's given name seems to me—freedom!"

"My name's Maurie."

The hoarseness of his voice was the music of the spheres.

"And mine is Jacqueline."

"It's a wonderful name!"

"Say it."

"Jacqueline!"

She looked up with childish curiosity.

"I have never heard it spoken that way before. It seems—it seems to me free—like your own wild west!"

"Ain't you been free?"

Her head fell. Her left hand pressed his in her effort to keep back the bubbling laughter. He returned the grip with a mighty interest.

"I have lived all my life in a convent!"

He started.

"I thought you was hangin' out along Fifth Avenue?"

It was a close squeeze. She blessed a sudden thundering on the slide trombone. All fat men have kind hearts, she decided.

"Yes, but only for a little while. Only for a few months. Then they brought me west."

                                     A SAGEBRUSH CINDERELLA

The last paragraph of a third instalment rose word by word before her eyes.

"They thought to bury me in the west! Even out here they guard me like a criminal! To-night I had to run away to be with you—you all. But they cannot bury me in this country. I look upon the stars at night and do not feel alone. The desert is my friend. I feel its mystery. And I feel the truth and strength of the men of the desert. Somewhere among them I shall find one friend!"

She bowed her head again.

"Some memory, Jac!" she was saying to herself.

The deep rumble of his voice, broken and passionate, broke in upon her.

"By God, you have found that friend. I'm him!"

"Mr. Gordon—Maurie!"

He could not speak!

The music stopped, and as it died away they caught a clear laugh from across the hall.

"The feller that come with you seems to be havin' a pretty fair sort of a time," said Maurie.

Jac looked up. There was Carrigan laughing heartily with Dolly Maxwell. She seemed extremely beautiful when she laughed, and her voice was musical—it rose over the babble of the dance hall like the chime of a bell. Jac set her teeth. She remembered the Carrigan Cut— as Maurie had failed to do it! Dave Carey was approaching.

"Here comes my next partner," she said, "but—"

Her pause said a thousand things. It made Maurie stand very straight. He was taking the burden of a woman's happiness upon his shoulders—and such a woman!

"I will never forget!"

The tensity of his emotion made him grammatical.

"Come with me, an' we'll sit out the dance. Send Carey away."

"But if he don't want to go?"

"I'll bust his jaw for him if he don't."

"Please—Maurie!"

"All right," he said, relenting slowly. "I'll see you later."

As he retreated, Jac turned to Dave Carey. He was standing stiffly, like a soldier awaiting orders.

"'I'll see you later!'" she quoted. "I wonder if I should consider that a promise or a threat, Mr. Carey? Or is it just a westernism?"

Dave Carey expanded. He knew that the girl in the fluffy pink dress was watching him with a white face.

"Poor ol' Maurie," he said gently. "He ain't much on manners. He was never given much of a bringin' up. Maybe you noticed it sort of in his way of talkin'. You're lookin' sort of sad."

She was gazing pensively on the happy faces of Dolly Maxwell and Carrigan. Now she lowered a gloomy eye to the floor.

"I try to seem gay, Mr. Carey."

"But there's somethin' eatin' on your mind?"

She looked up with childish admiration. "How could you tell? But you westerners see everything."

The clear music of Dolly Maxwell's laughter floated to her. Her brow clouded.

" I cannot help being unhappy, Mr. Carey."

Carey's hand slipped down on his hip and then he sighed. No one had been allowed to wear a six-gun into the dance-hall.

"Somebody botherin' you? P'int him out!"

"If there were, you would protect me, Mr. Carey, I know!"

"Would I!"

     A SAGEBRUSH CINDERELLA

"You've no idea how secure it makes me feel just to hear you speak that way."

"Honest?"

"Yes, for I know that you could keep danger and trouble far away from me."

He cleared his throat. His chest arched.

"Which I'd say I throw a six-gun about as fast as anybody in these parts."

"'Throw a six-gun,' Mr. Carey?"

"Sure," he explained. "Flash a six—pull a cannon—draw my revolver."

"Oh, Mr. Carey! Do you mean that you have ever drawn your revolver upon a man?"

"On a man? Me? I guess maybe you ain't heard any of the boys tell about me!"

"Oh, yes. Of course, I've heard a great deal about Dave Carey. You're the first man Mr. Carrigan pointed out to me when I came into the dance-hall."

"Is that straight? Well, Carrigan ain't a bad hand himself, I guess, but you can see by the way he handles himself that he ain't much in a fight."

"Can you tell simply by looking at a man?"

"Easiest thing in the world. Watch their hands. Look at big Maurie Gordon over there. Too big! All beef! No nerve! If him an' me was to mix, I'd fill him full of lead before he ever got his gun clear."

"Mr. Corey! You wouldn't shoot at poor Mr. Gordon?"

"He knows enough not to pick no trouble with me."

"Mr. Carey, somehow I feel that I can talk frankly to you!"

He swelled visibly. His face was red.

"Tag-dance!" bellowed the announcer.

Carrigan was rising to dance again with Dolly Maxwell. The solemn face of Ben Craig drew near. His stare was a promise as she started off with Dave Carey.

With the rehearsal on Maurie Gordon to help, she talked very smoothly now. She reached her great point: "But they cannot bury me in this country. I look upon the stars at night and do not feel alone. And I feel the strength and truth of the men of the desert. Somewhere among them I shall find—"

Here she noted Carrigan standing unemployed at the edge of the hall. He had been tagged quickly, of course, because of pretty Dolly Maxwell. She signaled him with a great appeal in her eyes and before they had taken half a dozen more steps his hand fell on the arm of Carey. As she slipped into the arms of Carrigan, her smile of farewell to Carey was sad and wistful. He stood stock still in the middle of the floor, jolted freely by the passing couples. In his eyes was a melancholy light of the sea-bound traveler who sees the last towers of his home port drop below the horizon.

CHAPTER VII

THE ROPING OF CARRIGAN

"Carey and Gordon roped, tied, and branded," said Carrigan. "But don't forget that powder puff."

"Carrigan, let me talk. I've been passing such a line of fancy lingo that my throat is dusty. I've been rememberin' everything that I ever read in love stories an' if I can't be myself for a minute I'll choke for want of fresh air."

"Thought you were having a pretty fair sort of a time," said Carrigan, absently.

His eyes were traveling over her head. She caught a glimpse of bright-haired Dolly Maxwell as they whirled. He was drifting away from her—that was plain.

"I've just been stringin' 'em along," said Jac. "But you're different, Carrigan!"

And here her eyes rose slowly to his. Far away she sensed the somber face of Ben Craig. She had not much time. Carrigan was looking down at her now.

"Look here," he said bluntly, "you can't tie every steer in the corral to one rope, Miss Silvestre. Keep the brandin' iron away from me. The fire ain't hot enough to hurt me yet. The iron won't make no mark."

Jac thought of Maude Merriam at the great moment when her husband tells her that he loves another woman. She caught her breath. She made her eyes grow wide. "Do you really think that I would—"

"Damn it, Jac, ain't Maurie and Carey enough for you? And there's Ben Craig lookin' at you like a wolf at a calf."

"Carrigan!"

The timbre of her voice made him start. She knew that he would not forget her to look after Dolly Maxwell for some time.

"Well?"

"Do you think I'm a flirt?"

"Jac, I'm warnin' you now. Don't feed me the spur no more. I'm the fairy godmother. I ain't the prince in the story."

"Is it all a story?"

He groaned.

"I thought I would find one man who wasn't just part of the fairy tale."

"There you go with your book English. Jac, you can't rope me. I see the shadow of the noose flyin' over my head an' I'm goin' to duck out from under."

She turned away with a far-off sorrow in her face.

"There's tears in your eyes!"

A pathetic smile quivered an instant at the corners of her lips.

"Honest, ain't you jest throwin' a rope, Jac?"

"I thought **you** would understand me, Carrigan."

He was breathing hard. She remembered a caption which had been flashed on a Maude Merriam screen.

"I thought you were **big** enough to understand!"

"My God!" whispered Carrigan.

"What?"

"The rope's on me!"

"Carrigan, why do you play with me like this?"

    A SAGEBRUSH CINDERELLA

"*Me* play with *you?*"

"Yes. Is it fair?"

The keen eyes searched her intently. She felt as the duellist felt when the rapier of a foe slithered up and down his steel. The violin started a run.

"The Carrigan Cut!" she cried.

He went through with it automatically. "No one can dance like you!" she whispered, as the hand of Ben Craig fell on Carrigan's arm, and as she moved away with the solemn-faced cow-puncher, she saw Carrigan standing as Dave Carey had done, with the faraway look, like a man who says farewell to everything that matters in his life.

Maurie Gordon and Dave Carey, their eyes fixed upon one object on the dancing-floor, came together at a corner of the hall. She drew closer. They started forward at the same time, then stopped and glared at each other with bitter understanding.

"Maurie," said Carey gently, "take my tip. Don't bother Miss Silvestre no more to-night. It won't bring you nothin'."

Maurie smiled from the deeps of his pity.

"Jacqueline," he said, with marked emphasis, "has found one man who understands her."

Carey shook his head slowly. He spoke carefully, as one would explain a difficult problem to a child. Jac was making the second circuit of the hall with Craig. She had reached the point: "But don't westerners as a rule call each other by the given name, Mr. Craig?"

"She's had a sad life, Maurie," said Carey, his eyes following the graceful vision in green. "You, with your bringin' up, you couldn't understand how to take to a swell girl like—"

He stopped, stiffening, and changed of face.

"I guess that'll hold you, Maurie. Did you see her smile at me?"

"Smile at you?" said Maurie with unutterable scorn. "Why, you poor sawed-off runt, that was all for me. She smiled at me like that before. They've tried to—to—bury her in the West, but she's found—"

"One real man!"

"Me!" said Maurie.

The music stopped.

"Maurie, aside from bein' a little thick in the head, you're a pretty straight feller in most ways. I don't want to see you make no fool out of yourself."

The smile of big Gordon came from an infinite distance, from a height of almost sacred compassion.

"Jacqueline and me," he said softly, "we understand. She's led a sad—what the hell!"

For as the dancers returned to their chairs, Harry During, lurching across the floor, stopped in front of Jacqueline. He had found it difficult to get dancing partners that evening and for consolation and excitement he had retreated to the bar and attended seriously and conscientiously to the matter of quenching his thirst. That thirst was deep-seated and it had taken him a long time to reach the seat of the dryness. Now, however, he had become convinced that he had done his duty by his parched insides, and he started toward the door to take horse and ride home. On the way a vision crossed his path—a vision in green, with a floating mist of dainty coloring over her shoulders. He paused to admire. He remained to stare.

If he had been sober he would have resumed his course with a shrug of the shoulders. But he was not sober. There was a film across his eyes and a mighty music swelling within him. Reason was gone, and only instinct remained. But the eyes of instinct are far surer than the eyes of reason. He moved closer with a shambling step. He leaned over his sister.

"It's Jac!"

He burst into Homeric laughter. Ben Craig rose slowly, a dangerous man and a known man in the mountain-desert. Even through the mists of "red-eye," Harry During sobered a little under the crushing pressure of the hand which fell on his shoulder. He pointed, grinning for sympathy.

　　　　　　　　　　　　　　　　A SAGEBRUSH CINDERELLA

"Look!" he said. "Ain't it funny? That's my shister! That's Jac!"

Craig turned for an instant's glance at Jac. She had not changed color. There was a grave but impersonal sympathy in her steady eyes.

She said: "Please don't hurt the poor fellow—Ben!"

Craig turned back to Harry.

"It's a disgrace," he said, "to let a drunk like you wander around insultin' helpless girls. By God, it's got to stop."

"My own shister—" protested Harry weakly.

"On your way!" thundered Craig, for he was conscious that many eyes were upon him.

Two formidable figures appeared on either side of him. They were Maurie Gordon, black of face with wrath, and Dave Carey, his lip lifted from his teeth like a wolf about to snarl. They were three formidable animals, facing the swaying figure of Harry. When men act under the eyes of a woman, the careful veil of civilization is lifted. The lovely Miss Silvestre was nearby. The three became ravening beasts.

"Out with him!" said Dave Carey.

"Move!" said Maurie.

"Start!" said Ben Craig.

But the same thing that made the hair of Jacqueline red made the blood of Harry hot.

"I'll see you damned first," he said thickly.

Instantly six iron hands gripped him. He was whirled, and, struggling vainly, borne across the floor toward the door. A universal clapping of hands came from the edges of the hall. It was understood that Harry had insulted the lovely stranger, and in the West, a woman, whether beautiful or ugly, **may** be treated with familiar words but **must** be treated with reverent thought.

At the very threshold of the door that led from the main hall into the little anteroom where guns and hats were piled, Harry managed to wriggle loose. The fury of his anger was sobering him a little and restoring the nerves to his muscular control. He broke loose with a curse and swung feebly, uncertainly, at the nearest of his prosecutors. Carey and Craig ducked to rush and grapple with Harry; but big Maurie, with the thought of Miss Silvestre and "real men" floating in his brain, drew back his sledge-hammer right fist and smashed it into the face of young During.

Harry pitched back through the door as if a dozen hands had thrown him. The three turned and made straight for Jac like three little boys returning to their mother for praise due to a virtuous act after a day of naughtiness and spankings. The women around the hall were silent. They had heard the dull thud as that fist drove home. The men applauded the murmurs. It was the custom to applaud Maurie Gordon.

But when the three reached Jac, she sat white of face and still of eye.

"This don't happen often," began Carey.

"I never see anything like it before," added Craig.

"Anyway," said Maurie complacently, "I've taught him a lesson."

A hard voice sounded at his shoulder. He turned to stare into the furious eyes of Carrigan. There was nothing bulky about the latter, but now, with his lean, almost ugly face white with anger and his gleaming eye, he seemed strangely dangerous.

CHAPTER VIII

THE THREE MUSKETEERS

"Gordon," he said, "you need a lesson yourself."

Maurie stepped back.

"What's eatin' you?" he frowned.

"You hit him when he couldn't hardly raise a hand," snapped Carrigan.

There was no mistaking it. He meant fight. It shone in his eyes like hunger. It tensed his muscles till he seemed crouching to spring like some beast of prey.

"Please!" cried Jac, and stepped in between them.

"Shut up and sit down!" said Carrigan.

And he pointed with a stern arm. She shrank back to the wall.

"By God," snarled Dave Carey, "you can't talk to girls like that, stranger!"

"Then come outside with me an' I'll talk to a man. You too, Gordon, you—"

A thrilling cry from many women made them all turn. In the door stood Harry During with the light gleaming on his long six-gun.

"Gordon," he called. "Git down an' crawl like the dirty dog you are!"

There was another flash of light on steel. It was the proprietor who had drawn, but he did not attempt to draw a bead on Harry During. His gun cracked; there was a clang of iron and a crash of glass as the big gasoline lamp went out; the hall was flooded with a semi-dark. And with the coming of the darkness fear rushed on the crowd. A stampede started for the door, but who could find the door in that chaos of struggling bodies and swinging shadows? Through the windows came the faint light of the early dawn.

"Jac!" cried Carrigan.

But tall Ben Craig was already beside her.

"Leave it to me!" he said reassuringly. "You didn't make no mistake when you picked me out. I'll show you that the mountain-desert's got one real man to make up for a lot of coyotes!"

"Wait!" she pleaded.

"Jac!" called Carrigan again.

"Here!"

"Don't trust to no one but me," said Craig.

"Then get me out of this mob."

"Follow me."

"I will if I can."

"Then—"

He picked her up and lunged forward through the crowd.

"Drop her!" commanded the voice of Carrigan.

"Not for ten like you."

He released Jac to turn and fight. A fist cracked home against his face, and he swung furiously. They grappled, and Craig felt as if he were fighting a steel automaton. The muscles his hands fell upon were rigid. The fist on his head and ribs beat a tattoo. Dave Carey had found Jac.

"Thank God!" he cried. "I thought you were lost. Trust to me. I'll see you through!"

Like Craig, he picked her up.

"I'll take you home if you'll go with me."

    A SAGEBRUSH CINDERELLA

"Anywhere out of this crowd!"

"Jac!"

"Here!"

A hand caught Carey by the shoulder and jerked him around. In the dim light he saw the convulsed face of Carrigan and dropped Jac to strike out with all his might. His blow landed on thin air and a hard fist smashed against his ribs. He went to the floor with a crash. But though his breath was half gone, he clung to his foe and struggled like a wildcat. Wild tales were told of Dave Carey in a fight. He lived up to all those stories now. But finally a clubbed fist drove against the point of his chin. He relaxed.

The burly shoulders of Maurie Gordon loomed through the semi-dark above Jac.

"Jacqueline!"

"Maurie!"

"Thank God I've found you!"

"Yes, thank God!"

"This way after me. There's the door!"

"Jac!"

"Here!"

And a demoniac sprang at Maurie through the dark.

Accustomed by this time to the dim light, the crowd was swirling rapidly through the door, and in the outgoing tide went Jac. The same confusion which made a hell of the dance-hall reigned in the open air. But there was more space to maneuver, and Jac gathered her gown up high and slipped through the crowd to the place at which Carrigan had tethered his horse.

She caught the pommel and swung up to the saddle like a man. There was a sickening sound of ripping and tearing. The green gown was hopelessly done for. She gave no thought to it, and landing astride in the saddle—a position which completed the ruin of the dress—she gave the horse his head and drove forward with a shout like that of a drunken cow-puncher.

And she was truly intoxicated with triumph. The men of her choice fought for her in the dance-hall. They were her knights battling for the smile of their lady. To one of them would go the victory, but hers was all the glory. She shouted at the coming dawn and urged the horse into a faster run. The wind caught at her face and whistled sharply past her ears—the song of victory!

No delay for the fording of the river! She took it on the run, splashed from head to foot with mud and water. She did not care. The gown was a wreck. Her hair tumbled down her shoulders. But she reached the further bank and drove on at a gallop, shouting like one of the Valkyrie.

A battle of giants waged in the dance-hall, where Maurie Gordon and Carrigan raged back and forth, sometimes standing at arm's length and slugging with both hands, sometimes grappling and punching at close range, sometimes rolling over and over on the floor and fighting every inch of the way.

If the great arms of Maurie gave him an advantage in the open fighting, the venomous agility of Carrigan evened matters when they came to close quarters.

Dave Carey drew himself up to a sitting posture with both hands pressed over his mid-ribs while he watched the conflict. Ben Craig leaned against the wall, sick and white of face. Through his swollen eyes he could barely make out the twisting figures. And still they slugged and smashed with a noble will, until, missing a swing at the same time, they were thrown to the floor by the wasted force of their own blows and sat staring stupidly at one another.

The growing daylight made them quite visible now. It showed two battered countenances. It showed equally torn clothes.

"Where's Jacqueline?" cried Maurie.

"Gone!" cried Carrigan, and started to his feet.

Gordon followed suit, but slowly. He was badly hurt in both body and mind. The two heroes stared at each other.

"Done for!" groaned Dave Carey from the distance.

"Stung!" sighed feeble Ben Craig.

"Beat!" growled Maurie.

"Roped!" said Carrigan.

"Fellers," said Carey, struggling to his feet, and still caressing his injured ribs, "I got an idea we better see that Fifth Avenue swell before we do more fightin'."

"I got to find her," said Gordon stoutly. "She depends on me. I'm the one real man she's ever known."

"You be damned before you find her," said Carrigan, and the light of battle flared in his eyes again.

"Hold on," interposed Carey. "You ain't the real man she's found. *I'm* it!"

"You are?" sneered Craig. "They tried to bury her in the West but she's goin' to be set free by a man who—"

"Who tried to bury her in the western desert?" asked Carrigan.

The other three spoke with one voice.

"Her uncle!" said Carey.

"Her cruel father," said Craig.

"Her older brother," said Maurie.

They turned and stared at each other, stunned. Once more they spoke in one voice.

"Stung!"

"I believe her." defended Maurie. "She's led a sad life in a convent all these years—"

"In a boarding-school, you mean," said Carey.

"Wrong; a girls' school," said Craig. They stopped again. Light from the dim distance was coming in their eyes.

And Jac, after leaving the down-headed horse in front of her father's hotel, stole swiftly up the stairs to her room.

"Who's there?" roared the familiar voice from Jim During's room.

"Me."

"Where've you been all night?"

"None of yer business."

"Jac, I'm goin' to raise the devil if you try many more of these funny tricks."

"I been out walkin'."

"All night?"

"Ain't I got a right to walk?"

"Jac, why wasn't you born a boy?" groaned old Jim, reverting to his old complaint.

"Because it's a lot more fun bein' a girl," said Jac, "when you've got the golden touch."

And she went into her room.

It was hard to look at herself in the faint light and with the little round pocket mirror which had been ample for all her needs before.

The glory of Cinderella was gone—quite gone! The green gown was a wretched travesty; her hair was a tumbled mass; only in her smile and her eyes there was a difference, a new light of power which, having once come to a woman, dies only with her death. Truly the victory was hers! She started to remove her clothes.

It was a long task, but finally they were rolled into a small bundle and tucked into a little corner. She put on her old clothes and carefully retied the hard knot in her hair. The fairy godmother was gone. She washed the powder from her face. Cinderella once more sat in the ashes.

She was rattling away at the stove, preparing to make the fire for breakfast, when a sound of singing down the road brought her to the window. There came another Three Musketeers. They were mounted—Porthos, Athos, and Aratnis. And before them walked the new D'Artagnan—Carrigan. And with one voice they sang.

It should have been a sad song, for as they came closer she saw that they were battered of face and torn of clothes. Yet their song was glad. Experience, whether good or bad, makes strong men rejoice.

They trooped into the dining-room.

"Chow!" they thundered in unison, and Jac stepped to the door.

As one man they gaped.

Big Maurie Gordon walked to her with a scowl, took her face between his hands, and stared into her eyes. His own were so swollen that he was looking out of the narrowest of slits.

"Where have I seen you?" he said.

"Maybe you been dreamin' about me, you big stiff!" said Jac amiably.

Maurie dropped his hands and turned away.

"Yep. A nightmare," he said.

"I got a start, too," growled Carey. "An' when I seen Jac I thought about—"

"Don't say it," broke in Craig. "It makes me see red."

"Hit the kitchen, Bricktop," said Maurie, "an' rustle some ham an' eggs—lots of 'em."

She smiled, and the expression changed her whole face. The Three Musketeers jumped and stared at her with a return of their first interest. The fairy godmother was waving the wand.

"This," said Jacqueline, "is worse than the convent."

"The devil!" groaned Maurie. "This ain't possible."

"When I came west," went on Jac with the same smile, "I thought that I should find one real man."

They listened with mouths agape. It was like watching base lead being transmuted before their eyes to gold.

Carrigan winked his one good eye. The other was black and puffed.

"And I have found one," said Jac.

And she winked at Carrigan.

"I can leave it to you," said Carrigan, "to lead me a real man's life."

THE END

www.ingramcontent.com/pod-product-compliance
Lightning Source LLC
LaVergne TN
LVHW041753190726
843493LV00008B/2607